Dr. Seuss

Hooray For Diffendoofer Day!

WITH SOME HELP FROM

Jack Prelutsky & Lane Smith

design by **Molly Leach**

ALFRED A. KNOPF · NEW YORK

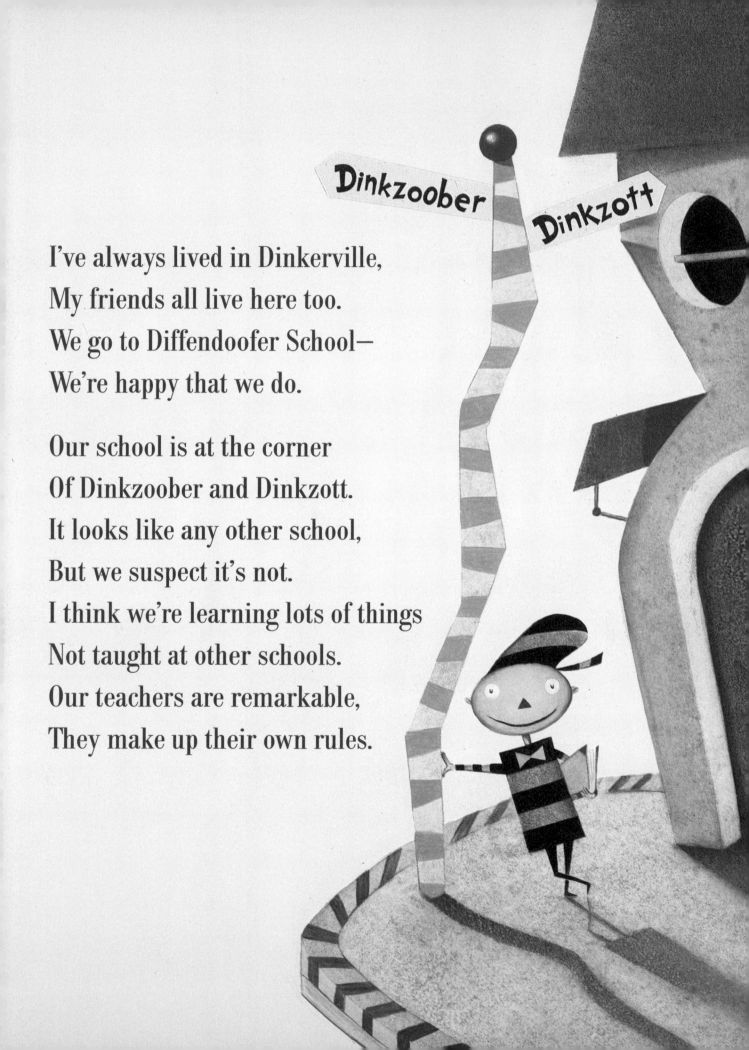

I've always lived in Dinkerville,
My friends all live here too.
We go to Diffendoofer School—
We're happy that we do.

Our school is at the corner
Of Dinkzoober and Dinkzott.
It looks like any other school,
But we suspect it's not.
I think we're learning lots of things
Not taught at other schools.
Our teachers are remarkable,
They make up their own rules.

Miss Bobble teaches listening,
Miss Wobble teaches smelling.
Miss Fribble teaches laughing,
And Miss Quibble teaches yelling.

Miss Twining teaches tying knots
In neckerchiefs and noodles,
And how to tell chrysanthemums
From miniature poodles.

Miss Vining teaches all the ways
A pigeon may be peppered,
And how to put a saddle
On a lizard or a leopard.

My teacher is Miss Bonkers,
She's as bouncy as a flea.
I'm not certain what she teaches,
But I'm glad she teaches me.

"Look! Look!" she chirps. "I'll show you how
To tell a cactus from a cow,
And then I shall instruct you why
A hippo cannot hope to fly."

She even teaches frogs to dance,
And pigs to put on underpants.
One day she taught a duck to sing—
Miss Bonkers teaches EVERYTHING!

Of all the teachers in our school,
I like Miss Bonkers best.
Our teachers are all different,
But she's *different-er* than the rest.

We also have a principal,
His name is Mr. Lowe.
He is the very saddest man
That any of us know.
He mumbles, "Are they learning
This and that and such and such?"
His face is wrinkled as a prune
From worrying so much.

He breaks a lot of pencil points
From pushing down too hard,
And many dogs start barking
As he mopes around the yard.
We think he wears false eyebrows.
In fact, we're sure it's so.
We've heard he takes them
      off at night…
I guess we'll never know.

But we *know* he likes Miss Bonkers,
He treats her like a queen.
He's always there to watch her
When she's on her trampoline.

There are many other people
Who make Diffendoofer run.
They are utterly amazing—
I love every single one.

Our nurse, Miss Clotte,
      knows what to do
When we've got sniffles or the flu.
One day I had a splinter, so
She bandaged me from head to toe.

Mr. Plunger, our custodian,
Has fashioned a machine—
A super-zooper-flooper-do—
It keeps the whole school clean.

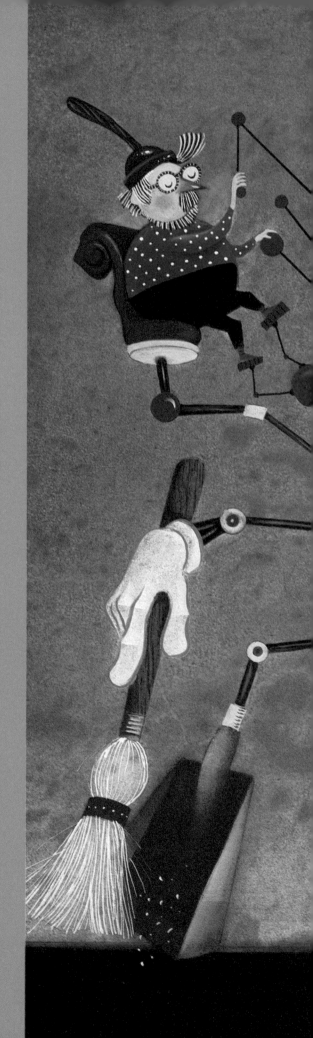

Our music teacher, Mrs. Fox,
Makes bagpipes out of
straws and socks.
Our art instructor, Mr. Beeze,
Paints pictures hanging by his knees.

In science class with Mr. Katz,
We learn to build robotic rats.

In gym we watch as Mr. Bear
Hoists elephants into the air.

Miss Loon is our librarian,
She hides behind the shelves,
And often cries out, "LOUDER!"
When we're reading to ourselves.

We have three cooks, all named McMunch,
Who merrily prepare our lunch.
They make us hot dogs, beans, and fries,
Plus things we do not recognize.
And as they cook, they sing their song,
Not too short and not too long.
"Roast and toast and slice and dice,
Cooking lunch is oh so nice."

Cafeteria
Gym
Art
Z-2
E-i-o
?
Hither
A-1
Dither
Nurse
G
10-X
L-7
Music
YONDER
Principal
30-G
Library
Girls
Boys

We were eating their concoctions,
Telling jokes and making noise,
When Mr. Lowe appeared and howled,
"Attention, girls and boys!"

He began to fuss and fidget,
Scratch and mutter, sneeze and cough.
He shook his head so hard, we thought
His eyebrows *would* come off.
He wrung his hands, he cleared his throat,
He shed a single tear,
Then sobbed, "I've something to announce,
And that is why I'm here.

"All schools for miles and miles around
Must take a special test,
To see who's learning such and such—
To see which school's the best.
If our small school does not do well,
Then it will be torn down,
And you will have to go to school
In dreary Flobbertown."

"Not Flobbertown!" we shouted,
And we shuddered at the name,
For *everyone* in Flobbertown
Does *everything* the same.

It's miserable in Flobbertown,
They dress in just one style.
They sing one song, they never dance,
They march in single file.
They do not have a playground,
And they do not have a park.
Their lunches have no taste at all,
Their dogs are scared to bark.

Miss Bonkers rose. "Don't fret!" she said.
"You've learned the things you need
To pass that test and many more—
I'm certain you'll succeed.
We've taught you that the earth is round,
That red and white make pink,
And something else that matters more—
We've taught you how to think."

"I hope you're right," sighed Mr. Lowe.
He shed another tear.
"The test is in ten minutes,
And you're taking it right here."

We sat in shock and disbelief.
"Oh no!" we moaned. "Oh no!"
We were even more unhappy
Than unhappy Mr. Lowe.
But then the test was handed out.
"Yahoo!" we yelled. "Yahoo!"
For it was filled with all the things
That we all *knew* we knew.

There were questions about noodles,
About poodles, frogs, and yelling,
About listening and laughing,
And chrysanthemums and smelling.
There were questions about other things
We'd *never* seen or heard,
And yet we somehow answered them,
Enjoying every word.

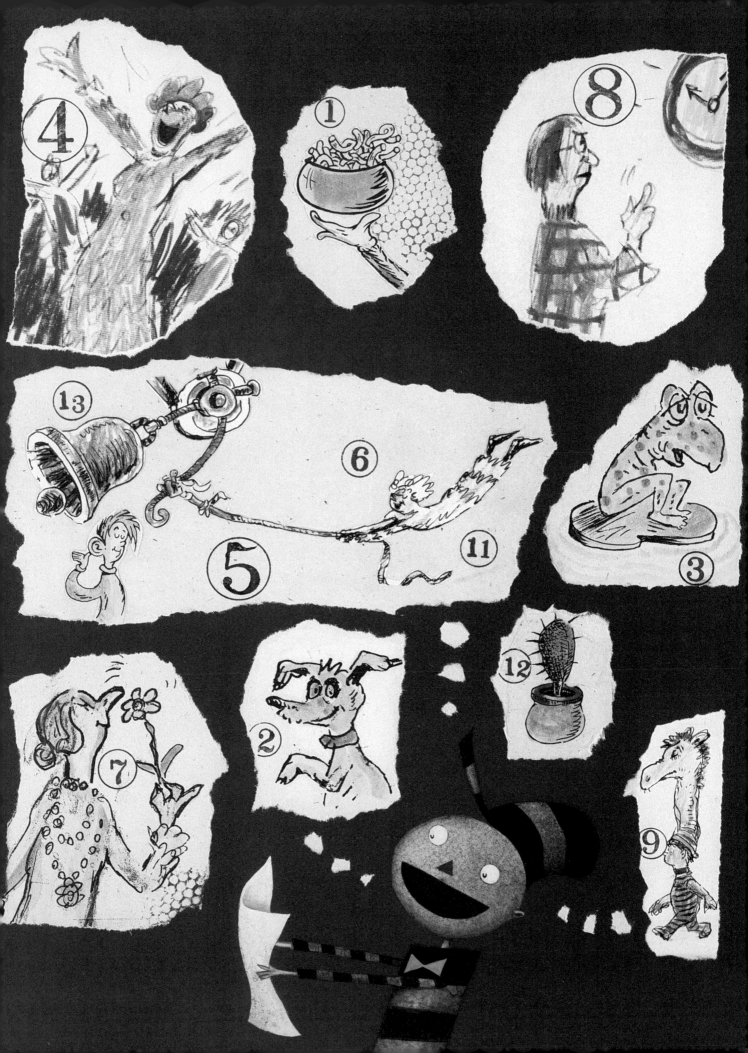

One week later, after recess,
Mr. Lowe meandered in.
We'd never seen him smile before,
But now he wore a grin.

He soon began to giggle,
Then his giggle grew by half,
And then it *really* happened—
Mr. Lowe began to laugh.

"You've saved our school!
You've saved our school!"
He jubilantly roared.
"We got the very highest score!"
He wrote it on the board.

Miss Bonkers did some cartwheels
Till her face turned cherry red.
She bounded up to Mr. Lowe
And kissed him on the head.
"Hooray! Hooray!" she shouted.
"I'm so proud I cannot speak."
So she did another cartwheel,
And she pecked him on the cheek.

"Ahem! Ahem!" coughed Mr. Lowe.
"You all deserve a bow.
I thus declare a holiday—
It starts exactly now.
Because you've done so splendidly
In every sort of way,
This day forever shall be known
As Diffendoofer Day.
And furthermore, I promise
I won't ever wear a frown.
For now I know we'll never go
To dreary Flobbertown."

Then we held a celebration,
There was pizza, milk, and cake.
Like everyone, I ate too much
And got a bellyache.
We laughed and whooped and hollered
The entire school day long,
Then we all sang, triumphantly,
"The Diffendoofer Song."

We love you, Diffendoofer School,
We definitely do.
There surely is no other school
That's anything like you.
You're *gribbulous*, you're *grobbulous*,
Each day we love you more.
You are the school we treasure
And unceasingly adore.

Oh, finest school in Dinkerville—
The only one as well—
We love you, Diffendoofer School,
Much more than we can tell.
You are so *diffendooferous*
It gives us joy to say,
Three cheers for Diffendoofer School—

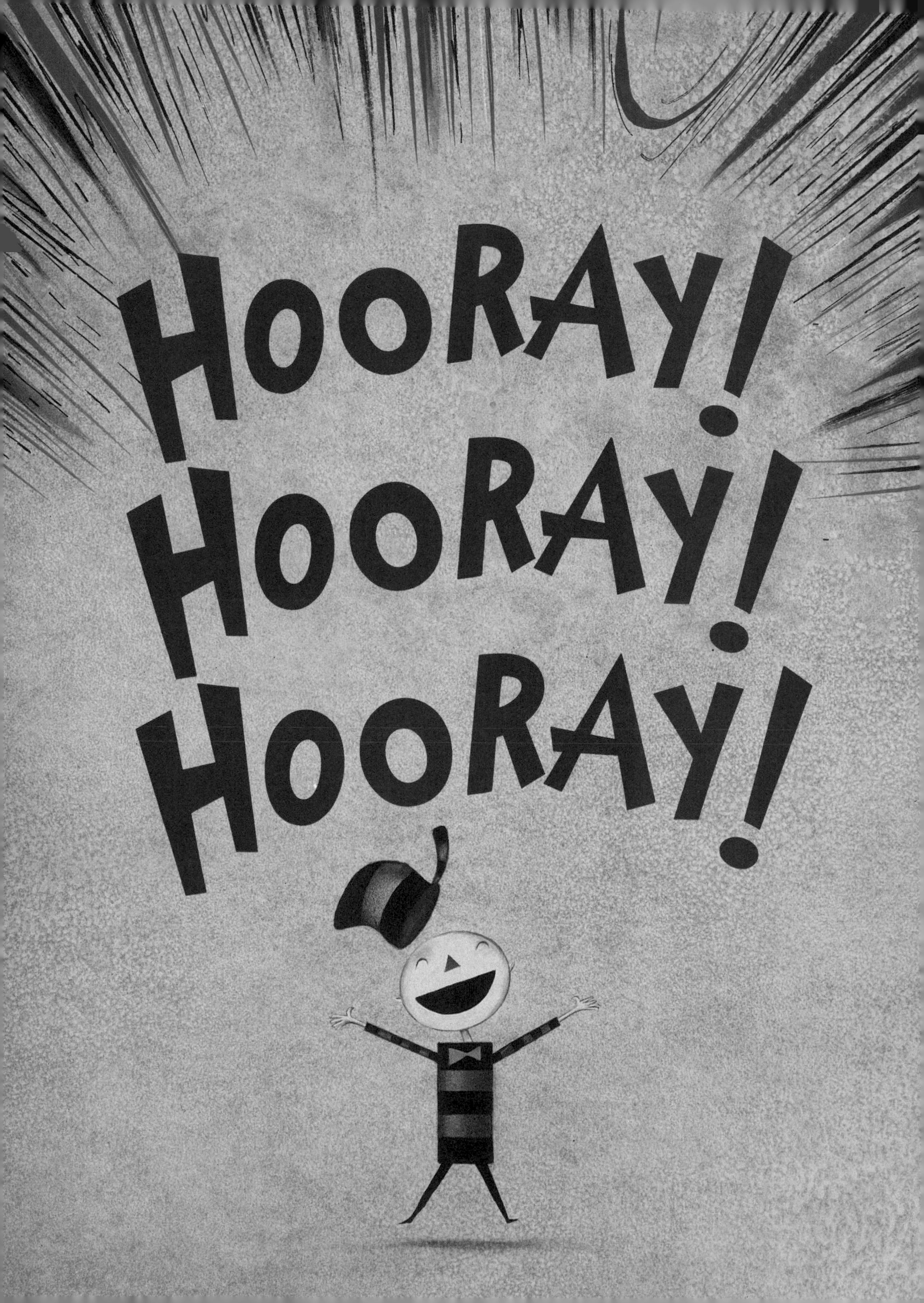
HOORAY!
HOORAY!
HOORAY!